s likes
to play games

92

Tas likes to play a game.

Tas likes to play with the pine cone.

The pine cone is in the garden near the rope.

Gem can see the pine cone near the rope.

Gem can hide the pine cone.

Tas likes to find the pine cone.

Tas likes to play with the rope.

Gem likes to pull the rope.

Tas likes to jump on the rope.

Tas can ride on the rope.

Tas can pull the rope too!

Tas likes this game.

Bec can see Tas and
Gem play.

Bec is happy to sit in the
pine tree.

Gem and Tas play a new game.

They will not play with the rope.

Tas and Gem will play with the pine tree.

The pine tree is wide and big.

Tas and Gem run around the big wide pine tree.

Gem and Tas are tired. Time to sleep.